The Milliner

by

Suzanne Glass

SAMUEL FRENCH

FOUNDED 1830

NEW YORK HOLLYWOOD LONDON TORONTO

SAMUELFRENCH.COM

ISBN **978-0-573-66032-0**   Printed in U.S.A.   #14839

IMPORTANT BILLING AND CREDIT REQUIREMENTS

All producers of THE MILLINER mu*st* give credit to the Author of the Play in all programs distributed in connection with performances of the Play, and in all instances in which the title of the Play appears for the purposes of advertising, publicizing or otherwise exploiting the Play and/or a production. The name of the Author *must* appear on a separate line on which no other name appears, immediately following the title and *must* appear in size of type not less than fifty percent of the size of the title type.

EAST 13TH STREET THEATER

The Directors Company
Michael Parva, Artistic/Producing Director
in association with
Milliner Productions

Presents the World Premiere of

The Milliner

a new play by
Suzanne Glass

with

Michel Gill

Julia Haubner   Caralyn Kozlowski

Maria Cellario   Donna Davis   Steven Hauck   Glenn Kalison

scenic design	costume design	lighting design
Todd Edward Ivins	**Gregory Gale**	**Jeff Nellis**

projection design	sound design	music direction/original music
Brian H. Kim	**Nick Borisjuk**	**Warren Wills**

lyric translation	casting	fight director
Alick Glass	**Stuart Howard, Amy Schecter, & Paul Hardt**	**Rick Sordelet**

wig and hair design	hats created by
Carole Morales	**Lynne Mackey**

production manager	production stage manager	company manager
B.D. White	**Melissa M. Spengler**	**Katherine Heberling**

press representatives	marketing	general manager
O & M **Origlio/Miramontez Co.**	**Leanne Schanzer** **Promotions**	**Gindi Theatrical** **Management**

directed by
Mark Clements

 This production is made possible with public funds from the New York State Council on the Arts, a state agency

with the support of
The Lucille Lortel Foundation

CHARACTERS

WOLFGANG GEORG. Mid-late 40's. Handsome, sexy, charismatic. Jewish, though not obviously so in appearance. A complex, multi-layered character.

AMALIA GEORG. Wolfgang's wife. 30's. Dark-haired, attractive, sensitive, worldly and pragmatic.

CLAUDIA. 30's. Owns and runs a fashionable milliner's boutique in Berlin. A sometimes cabaret singer. Blonde, sexy and Aryan in appearance. A strong Dietrich style voice. Confident, flirtatious and with a surface affability that conceals a far darker side to her nature.

WOLFGANG'S MOTHER. Late 40's/early 50's. A refined Berliner. Strong willed and sensitive.

FRAU HENDEL. Early 50's. An attractive gentile Berliner.

GERHARDT MÜLLER. 30's. Blonde and Aryan looking. Charming in a very Germanic way.

MAX . Concierge. 40's/50's. Warm natured and friendly.

HEINZ. 40's. Claudia's friend. Jovial and affable.

PAUL. 40's Claudia's Friend. Reserved.

AUTHOR'S FOREWORD.

In desperation, in the psychiatrist's chair, my main character Wolfgang says, "Not everyone, can be as strong as having their roots ripped out from under them as my wife. Some of us can no longer find any hat that fits. And it hurts Doctor... it's quite literally pain for home ... And you feel so alone. You can't see yourself reflected in anybody's eyes." Wolfgang's expression is the essence of my play. I wanted to depict a man, who, despite Nazi persecution, continued to see Germany as his "home". Only at home could he make beautiful hats, play Brahms with feelings, savour the pleasures of his life. Even in the face of Nazi threats, Wolfgang is unwilling to let go of Berlin, until he is almost coerced by others to flee to England, leaving his beloved mother behind. Still he staunchly refuses to deny his German identity and adapt to his new British neighbors. His love for his homeland means he can acknowledge neither it's cruelty nor his mother's probable fate in a death camp. My intention is that Wolfgang's emotional struggle and adamant denial shed 20light on the torment of being torn from the only home one knows and loves. The need to feel the ground of home beneath our feet surely belongs to all of us.

Suzanne Glass, October 2008.

I dedicate this play to the memory of my Grandfather, William Wollenberg, a milliner, a gentleman, a pianist and above all a Berliner.

I dedicate it too to my Grandmother Eva and to my parents...to my Mother, the milliner's daughter and to my Father, my lyricist and the first to read the part of Wolfgang.'

ACT 1

(WOLFGANG GEORG sits on a wooden bench in a Berlin prison cell. The year is 1948. He wears a dark suit and tie and holds a trilby in his hand. A shaft of light shines onto his face.

He is a handsome upright man in his late 40's. Behind and above him several outsized stylish colorful hats are suspended in the blackness. A tall blonde sexy woman enters. She begins to sing "Mother Have You Forgiven Me?" in German, then in English.)

CLAUDIA.

> MUTTER HAST DU MIR VERGEBEN?
> MUTTER DENKST DU NOCH DARAN?
> MUTTER HAST DU MIR VERGEBEN?
> WAS ICH DIR ANGETAN?
>
> MY COUNTRY CAN YOU NOW FORGIVE ME ?
> MY COUNTRY DOES HURT STILL REMAIN?
> MY COUNTRY AM I NOW FORGIVEN?
> FOR CAUSING YOU SUCH PAIN?
>
> MOTHER CAN YOU NOW FORGIVE ME?
> MOTHER DOES HURT STILL REMAIN?
> MOTHER..

(Lights fade on the singer.)

WOLFGANG. I still feel like a milliner you know. It never leaves you.

My fingers dream of making hats like the drinker craves the burn of a whisky. I got the passion from my Mother. She was crazy about hats.

"Wolfgang, the tilt of the brim has to sit just right. Just like this. The grain of the velvet has to lie just right.

Just like that." She was such a perfectionist when it came to dressing people's heads.

And every season she'd make a hat for herself too.

She wasn't a vain woman. But she knew *exactly* what suited her. She went for reds and oranges...Not a muted orange. But a sort of...a sort of *blood* orange. My aunt wrote to me, that even when my Mother was in the camp, she had smuggled in her...orange felt beret. The one she used to wear tilted to the side. *(Struggles with his composure)* She'd take it out of the drainpipe and she'd sleep in it, my aunt told me. When she could. I mean...when she slept...Imagine that, Mother, with a shaved head in her orange beret. Anyway as I said she was crazy about hats. My mother. *(Pause)* And so am I... Still crazy about hats. (**WOLFGANG** *plays with the hat.*)

(In the milliner's showroom circa 1916. The showroom doubles as a workshop with a workbench. In the corner there is a small-decorated Christmas tree. Wolfgang's **MOTHER** *works cutting orange felt on a wooden block for a beret.)*

MOTHER. Wolfgang! Wolfgang! Wolfgang, have you practiced your pieces?

WOLFGANG. Yeeees. Now can I work with you Mama?

MOTHER. Of course sweetheart. Come here.

WOLFGANG. Mama.

MOTHER. Yes.

WOLFGANG. Mama.

MOTHER. Yes Wolfgang.

WOLFGANG. In the changing room today...

MOTHER. Yes?

WOLFGANG. My friends laughed at me.

MOTHER. *(Focuses on the cutting)* Oh? Why?

WOLFGANG. My penis.

MOTHER. They've all got one haven't they? All the boys.

WOLFGANG. Yes, but they said mine had a hat on it. And I looked and it does Mama. They said you and Papa cut it. *(Mother sighs)*

Did you Mama? Did you cut it?

MOTHER. A special man did Wolfgang. He didn't exactly cut it. He snipped it…The skin, I mean, not the actual…

WOLFGANG. Snipped it? Like how much? Show me how much.

MOTHER. Just a tiny bit.

WOLFGANG. Show me how much.

MOTHER. For God's sake child. Just about…that much. *(Snips a tiny piece off the felt)* And you had wine afterwards. A vintage red, I remember. We put a drop to your lips. Your father had brought it back from Paris. I said, at eight days old you probably wouldn't notice the difference between a vintage and a cheap wine, but he insisted on opening it. *(She babbles)* That's probably where you got the taste for it. Wolfgang, maybe tonight you can have a sip from my glass.

WOLFGANG. Why did you let the man do that to me Mama?

MOTHER. To keep you clean and healthy.

WOLFGANG. It was a stupid thing to do to me…It's not a hat you know, Mama…You can't throw it away if you do it wrong.

MOTHER. I don't think he did it wrong, Wolfgang. And get off the hatbox please.

WOLFGANG. How do you know he didn't do it wrong?

MOTHER. He'd been doing it for years. That's all he does.

WOLFGANG. Uhhh! That's the worst job in the world. Uhhh!!

MOTHER. *(Laughs)* At least you're clean.

WOLFGANG. I don't want to be clean. I want to be the same as my friends.

MOTHER. Maybe it was foolish Wolfgang. *(Mutters to herself)* He made things too obvious…Some of your Father's ideas were, well…I still miss his stupid ideas. But parents can do stupid things too you know Wolfgang…

like smothering their children. Someone should give us black marks for bad behavior like you get at school... *(As if to herself)* At least we'd see where we were going wrong before our children start to blame us....Now come. Let's get this beret finished in time for Christmas. *(She presses the felt she has cut over the block)* It's going to be the finest beret *Unter den Linden.* You'll see.

*(**MOTHER** begins to hum first line and then sing "Solang Untern Linden" in English.)*

MOTHER.

HERE BENEATH THE LINDEN THE OLD TREES BLOOM AGAIN,

NOTHING CAN EVER CHANGE WHEN BERLIN IS STILL BERLIN.

WHEN YOU CAN TRUST NO OTHER MY TRUST IS EVERGREEN,

YOU ARE MY OLDEST LOVER BERLIN IS STILL BERLIN.

YOU ARE MY OLDEST LOVER BERLIN IS STILL BERLIN.

*(The continuous wailing of a siren can be heard in the background. **WOLFGANG** in suit and tie as opening scene.)*

WOLFGANG. I couldn't wait for that sound from the London skies. I'd go and bury myself in the air raid shelter with my wife at the bottom of the garden. Amalia would paint by candlelight and I'd read my Goethe poems. Down there you were wherever you wanted to be...It was better than sleep. Falling asleep sometimes felt... Well...one had no control over the demons. But then the danger of blitz would be over and I'd get dragged back out. *(He squints remembering)* Poor Amalia...She had to drag me everywhere...If only I'd listened to her...She knew...But it's just that I had no desire to keep going to these ghastly gatherings...to sit at high tea with tortured refugees, who one minute said they'd integrated into English society without so much as a hiccup and the next started wailing for home. Sometimes, to prove a point they'd serve "Herringsalat" and Earl Grey *together*. The tastes declared war on my tongue.

Anyway they'd sit and gossip about the "friends" who hadn't been invited, then invite them the next time and dissect the previous lot. They were just so…so… Jewish.

(The lighting dims. **WOLFGANG** *puts on his Trilby.)*

As for the English, with their cocktail parties and their whiskey-flavoured water. They liked to think of themselves as hat people, but they spray so much starch on their hats, the things could walk off on their own. And as for the British Judges, they have the most unusual taste of all, especially when it comes to their headdresses…"Your honor this, your honor that" Your honor must be joking with that hat. *(To himself)* Probably better after all for me to go through this…this trial…in Berlin. At least I won't be offended by people's heads. Anyway, our English gentile neighbors invited us once. A gesture of welcome to their country, they said. *(Beat)* We'd been in our house for a year. *(Takes off his hat.)*

The room was full of upper-crust types who kept calling me "Wolfgang." *(W pronounced the English way)* I said, "No, no, it's Wolfgang. V, V, V - Wolfgang as in 'Aufwiedershen.'" "Ah, you are a real German, aren't you?" *(He laughs as they had done, imitating them.)* "A miller?" one of them said. And I said, no, no I wasn't a miller, but that you just had to insert the 'in' into miller and you got a milliner. That's what I am, I said. A hat maker, not a bread maker. The man said, "Ah, so you're a plain old hat salesman then…Patricia, Patricia!" A handsome woman came over. She started to say how she urgently needed a hat for her friend's wedding…Then she stopped me mid-sentence and stared at me. "Am I hearing things? That can't possibly be a German accent you have there can it?" Her husband explained I was a German Jew. She turned and walked away. *(pause)* And their friend muttered something about us all being tarred with the same brush…"Jews,

German Jews, Jewish Germans, we were all 'BF's'...
Bloody Foreigners." He said they'd let too many of the
damned people in and that compassion would be the
ruination of the British.

(WOLFGANG puts on his hat and leaves.)

(Change of lighting. He continues to reminisce.)

WOLFGANG. "Wolfgang, you are the sculptor and the ladies
heads are putty in your hands." In Berlin I was never
just a hat salesman. I was a *Hutmacher.* I still find the
German language beautiful...*Hut....Macher.* Maker,
creator of hats. So much more...logical. So much
more...beautiful. *(He looks down, plays with the hat in
his hand.)* Haute couture was my passion. You know
the sort of fashion I mean. The kind that the sound
of high heels on parquet floors and the scent of good
perfume bring to mind.

The English do try, but they just haven't got panache.
It all looks so planned with them. Oh yes, of course
there's beauty in their Ascot apparitions, but most of
them are imports from Europe. Anyway, the English are
not Europeans. Never will be. They can't just dress in a
heart beat like Germans can and look "comme il faut."

(Change of lighting. Purple, deep pink, indigo blue.

Velvet and satin hats and swathes of material lie around.
WOLFGANG *goes up to one of several hat stands, maneu-
vers the hat on its head.* **FRAU HENDEL** *enters. She is in
her early fifties, a stylish Gentile.)*

FRAU HENDEL. Ah! Here he is. The heir to the hat empire.
Hello Wolfgang. Your Mother promises me you will
look after me even better than she does.

WOLFGANG. She's a hard act to follow.

FRAU HENDEL. Yes, and a lovely person too. It's remarkable
the way she built up this business. You know, we always
end up in conversation about our children when she's
fitting my hats.

WOLFGANG. Ah, you do, do you? And what does my mother

say about me?

FRAU HENDEL. You don't need to ask me that, Wolfgang. You know you're the apple of her eye. You're all she's got. But I will tell you she won't be happy if you spend all your time talking to me instead of selling me a hat. *(Looking around)* Aah! I can almost smell the creativity in here.

WOLFGANG. *(Gestures her to sit)* Relax for a moment, Frau Hendel. *(Goes over to a tray decked with fine china)* Would you care for a little cup of coffee and a slice of my mother's delicious *Apfelstrudel?*

FRAU HENDEL. Thank you, but no. I have to fit into a very small evening dress next month.

WOLFGANG. I hear your son is getting married and you want something splendid. Actually you look far too young to be a mother-in law. And women would die for your complexion.

FRAU HENDEL. *(Plays with her hair)* You really think so?

(He selects a dramatic hat with an upturned brim on one side. He gently takes her hands, pulls her up and adjusts the hat on her head. She walks over to a full length mirror. She let's out a slight gasp, then laughs.)

FRAU HENDEL. I couldn't!

WOLFGANG. Because?

FRAU HENDEL. Well I might…

WOLFGANG. Upstage the bride?

FRAU HENDEL. Not exactly…but…

WOLFGANG. Are you fond of your future daughter-in-law?

FRAU HENDEL. Well, she's…she's…

WOLFGANG. Frau Hendel, I don't need to tell you how you look in that hat, do I?

*(**FRAU HENDEL** laughs, flattered.)*

WOLFGANG. I won't talk you into it though. Making your own choice is delicious.

*(**FRAU HENDEL** turns from the mirror to look at him, the*

hat still on her head.)

FRAU HENDEL. You're a bit of a philosopher aren't you, Wolfgang? How old are you if I might ask?

WOLFGANG. Oh, I'm er....I'm twenty six, but I wouldn't exactly call myself a philosopher. I do love working with women though. They have...they have a greater willingness to engage. Now, how about colour?

FRAU HENDEL. Well, if we're opting for drama how about fuchsia?

WOLFGANG. *(Laughs)* Perfect. Fuchsia felt with a small lace veil. Lace is the caviar of the fashion world these days. Actually I have another customer, a Frau Goering... you might know her. She has an order in for some lace. I could combine your orders.

FRAU HENDEL. Frau Goering? I see...Not the same colour as mine though, Wolfgang?

WOLFGANG. No, no, of course not. She said she wanted something to match her skin tone. We chose a shade of green. *(Beat)*
She wants to wear it for an orchestral concert and make her husband proud to have her on his arm.

FRAU HENDEL. I see.

WOLFGANG. She was telling me her theories about milliners last week. She maintains that the fibres in the felt can send you crazy. The mad milliner. *(He laughs)* The mad hatmaker, huh? She was quite offended when I made light of her ideas. I had to play her Brahms to appease her.

FRAU HENDEL. Now you know perfectly well you're not going to get away with that, don't you, Wolfgang? I refuse to be treated like a second-class citizen. I insist on hearing a little Brahms too.

WOLFGANG. Now? I couldn't, I...

FRAU HENDEL. I'm waiting Wolfgang. I might even invite you to join your Mother and me at the Philharmonic next month if I'm suitably impressed.

WOLFGANG. *(Crosses to the piano)* You, Madame, know precisely how to get round me.

(The room grows darker. He sits and begins to play Brahms' 'Hungarian Rhapsody No. 5'. FRAU HENDEL leaves. Wolfgang's MOTHER enters, dressed in a simple black dress and orange beret. She takes a seat, and listens to WOLFGANG from the other side of the room. He plays with skill. When he has finished she claps. He looks up, surprised.)

WOLFGANG. Mother, I didn't see you come in.

MOTHER. That was quite wonderful. Your Father would have been so proud of you. *(Bows her head)* We just need to find you a wife who enjoys that talent of yours…Father would have wanted that for you.

WOLFGANG. I'm always here for you, Mother. You do know that don't you?

MOTHER. I know. I know. Though I struggle with that, Wolfgang. I ought to let you go a little. Now play that piece again for me. Please.

(He sits and begins to play. After a few phrases the music fades and is picked up again on the gramophone of a living room in a London suburb in 1939. AMALIA, his wife, sits with a book in her hand. She is in her early forties, a dark beauty. An easel with a half painted picture of a face stands in the corner. AMALIA pours over a book of English grammar.)

AMALIA. Wolfgang, please put the music down. I can't concentrate. *(He sits there almost in a trance. Amalia recites from her book)* I love. You love. He loves. I loved. You loved. Wolfgang put it down!

WOLFGANG. *(Half joking)* I can't hear you.

AMALIA. Turn it off! Please!

(WOLFGANG walks over to her. She carries on reciting.)

AMALIA. You Love. We Love. They love.

WOLFGANG. *(Puts the music down)* You love what?

AMALIA. You, but leave me. I need to study.

WOLFGANG. For what?

AMALIA. *(Ignores him) I* would love. He would love. You would love.

WOLFGANG. If you loved me you would stop with those goddamned verbs.

AMALIA. They would love. We would love.

WOLFGANG. Let's go for a walk.

AMALIA. I would have loved.

WOLFGANG. What are you trying to prove Amalia?

(She looks at him pained. Half closes her book)

WOLFGANG. Why are you doing this? Why don't you paint instead?

AMALIA. We can't enjoy life here without good English grammar Wolfgang.

WOLFGANG. Enjoy life? Here? What's to enjoy…the glorious weather? The fine cuisine? The exquisite sense of fashion and grooming?

AMALIA. Wolfgang!

WOLFGANG. The open friendly people? The warm welcome we've received?

AMALIA. Please.

WOLFGANG. Please, what?

AMALIA. We're here.

WOLFGANG. With a bunch of grey faced introverts with defective taste chromosomes.

AMALIA. But we're here.

WOLFGANG. They don't want us.

AMALIA. They let us in.

WOLFGANG. Kind of them.

AMALIA. They let us stay.

WOLFGANG. Unfortunately.

AMALIA. The alternative would have been delightful.

WOLFGANG. It's too damp here; my joints didn't ache like this at home. And nothing works properly in this country.

AMALIA. There's a war on for God's sake.

WOLFGANG. That has nothing to do with it.

AMALIA. Wolfgang, this is it. Who cares if we don't have silver salt shakers? We're alive. *(She shakes his shoulders)* This is *it* Wolfgang. *(Loud whisper)* This is home now.

WOLFGANG. Yes, Amalia.

AMALIA. It has to be. Please.

WOLFGANG. No. I can't bear it for you either.

AMALIA. I'm fine, Wolfy. There is nowhere else now.

WOLFGANG. There's Berlin.

AMALIA. Are you crazy? You're losing your mind.

WOLFGANG. Am I?

AMALIA. *(She bends her head over her textbook)* I left. He left. She left. We left.

WOLFGANG. Come. Let's go for a walk before it's too late. It's getting dark.

(AMALIA ignores him)

Amalia, I said let's go…Amalia!

(AMALIA begins to sob. WOLFGANG walks up to her, puts his hands on her shoulders, strokes her hair, kisses the crown of her head.)

WOLFGANG. I'm sorry. I'm sorry.

(He encourages her to get up and leads her over to the old dresser with hooks for hats above the mirror. He takes a cornflower blue cloche [bell shaped hat] from one of the hooks, puts it on her head. He tilts it one way, then another. He stands behind her at the mirror. There is a moment of tenderness between them.)

WOLFGANG. Our joint creation. Do you remember?

(AMALIA nods.)

(Back to the showroom in Berlin. Their first meeting. Again swathes of coloured materials lie everywhere. He is gently flirtatious.)

WOLFGANG. *(With a peacock blue hat)* Fraulein, this is *your* hat.

AMALIA. *(Looks around her)* Where does one begin?

WOLFGANG. This one will suit you perfectly.

AMALIA. Not quite.

WOLFGANG. So, what can I offer you then? Raspberry mohair? Emerald silk? Sky blue satin? Midnight blue lace?

AMALIA. This is breathtaking Herr Georg. You live in a rainbow. These are...absolutely gorgeous. But for myself. I think I'd prefer something a little more low key.

WOLFGANG. Low key in your twenties? Now come Fraulein. What will you wear at 30? Donkey Grey? At 40? Widow's black? At 50? A sack over your lovely face perhaps?

(AMALIA laughs again.)

WOLFGANG. We could compromise a little.

AMALIA. How so?

WOLFGANG. A sage green? *(Puts his hand up as if to correct himself)* No, no that's still too old.

AMALIA. Chocolate brown perhaps.

WOLFGANG. Sunflower yellow.

AMALIA. A shade of beige.

WOLFGANG. Gold.

AMALIA. No, no not gold, but hazel.

WOLFGANG. *(WOLFGANG contemplates)* Hazel green might do it. To match your eyes. *(AMALIA looks down. WOLFGANG moves closer with two hats in his hand.)* We have to try on different shapes. The shape might dictate the colour.

AMALIA. Yes, yes, I know that from my painting. When the sea's angry you can't paint it turquoise and when it's calm it's such a shame to paint it grey. It's a waste of serenity if you know what I mean. I'm sorry I'm babbling. I...

WOLFGANG. No, no not at all. So you're an artist?

AMALIA. I paint, that's all. I don't think you can really call yourself an artist till there's a body of work to look back on. I've had only one exhibition.

WOLFGANG. Ah. Where was that?

AMALIA. In Paris.

WOLFGANG. Paris. Impressive. Almost as beautiful as Berlin.

AMALIA. More beautiful I would say…Take the *Sacré Coeur*.

WOLFGANG. The *Gedachtnisskirche* is more beautiful.

AMALIA. The *Opera du Paris* takes your breath away.

WOLFGANG. The *Staats Oper* beats it any day

AMALIA. And the *Seine*.

WOLFGANG. The *Spree* has more twists and turns.

AMALIA. *(They both laugh)* Alright, Herr Georg. I see you are a lost cause. *(Looks round the room)* You know I've just had one art exhibition, but you've had many.

WOLFGANG. I'm sorry?

AMALIA. Well I was thinking. Each of your hats is a work of art in its own right and when a woman walks down the street in it, it's like, like a moving exhibition. Although of course she could behave quite appallingly in your hat.

WOLFGANG. That's a terrifying thought!

AMALIA. I think I'd like to be reincarnated as the hat on the head of a fabulously wealthy woman. Then I could travel the world with her.

WOLFGANG. Ah, I see you're a wanderer.

AMALIA. I want to live in so many different places. Paris, London, Rome…And you?

WOLFGANG. Now and again it's fine to travel. Broadens the mind. But I have everything I love here. My music. My work. My people. It's all about the people isn't it? Besides, there's my Mother. She's very rooted here. I could never think of leaving her. *(Breaks off, looks* **AMALIA** *in the eye)*
Tell me, Fraulein, what do you paint?

AMALIA. People.

WOLFGANG. Classic portraits?

AMALIA. No not exactly. How to best describe it? I suppose I paint people from the inside out.

WOLFGANG. And how does that look? A kidney here? A bladder there?

AMALIA. No, certainly not. No, I suppose you could call my paintings fingerprints of people's faces. I paint the abstract of their faces in the shade each person brings to my mind. I think we each have our own predominant colour and deep down everybody knows which colour they are.

WOLFGANG. What colour am I then?

AMALIA. You? Now let's see…You're more of a tone than a color. A grey. *(Contemplating him)* But don't misunderstand me…I think grey is the most interesting. And I'd say you could go lighter or darker depending on what's happening around you.

WOLFGANG. I'd say that *you* are a sun kissed yellow…actually, you look a bit like my mother when she was young. She was very beautiful.

AMALIA. I can imagine.

WOLFGANG. Now how about this hat of yours? We need to spend some time to get the shape and the colour right.

AMALIA. *(Looks at her watch)* I don't believe it. My Mother will be waiting at the street corner. I'll have to come back another day.

WOLFGANG. If your Mother lets you.

AMALIA. Yes, if she does. She's a little over protective. Jewish Mothers.

WOLFGANG. I wouldn't know.

AMALIA. Oh you're not. I thought you were. I…

WOLFGANG. Not what?

AMALIA. I mean, I just assumed. The friends who recommended you. I was sure they said…

WOLFGANG. Said what?

AMALIA. That you were…

WOLFGANG. That I was?

AMALIA. Well, of the faith….

WOLFGANG. I never think about it. I mean by birth I am. But that's irrelevant. I've been baptized. I'm a German. No, no I'm a Berliner by religion.

AMALIA. Baptized?

WOLFGANG. Yes. Of course.

AMALIA. But why?

WOLFGANG. Because… because …..my parents wanted it I suppose. It's quite common you know. You seem so shocked.

AMALIA. Oh… Er… maybe.

WOLFGANG. You can tell your Mother, if it helps, *(Lowers his voice to a whisper)* I'm circumcised too...

AMALIA. Herr Georg!

WOLFGANG. If that means you're allowed to come back again…

WOLFGANG. Now go and find your mother and think about hazel green.

(AMALIA turns to go.)

WOLFGANG. Tomorrow then?

AMALIA. Tomorrow.

WOLFGANG. And think about the perfect shape of hat.

AMALIA. I'll paint it.

(WOLFGANG kisses her hand. She smiles and turns to go.

WOLFGANG sits on the bench. Addresses the audience as if teaching them about his art.)

WOLFGANG. You can tell so much about a woman from the hats that she wears. The idea that a hat acts as a symbol of modesty just because it covers your hair is nonsense. It can be more a sign of irreverence than of reverence.

A hat lets you play with nature and tease it. In my view it can be an expression of a woman's sexuality rather than a suppression of it.

I've always said hats and heels are a give away. I mean you can't exactly imagine a woman in a pillbox hat being highly…How should I put it? Being very open to exploring can you? But a large brim with a tantalizing feather trim perhaps and tapered ankles in a pair of stilettos say wonderful things about her. I can usually tell the minute a woman walks in what she's going to want on her head. Although what she thinks she wants at first isn't always what she really wants in the end. She might just be shy or repressed. And it's quite *beautiful* really the way you can see a woman change with the hat you put on her head. She might come in looking sad and asking for a beige beret and you look at her and see a certain spark, a certain something that's half extinguished by life and you coax and cajole her to look at a crimson velvet creation instead. And she tilts her head one way, then another. Adds a little lipstick…Just to see. She comes *alive*. And before you know it she's strutting. And the next season she comes back and asks for something bold herself. And you say, "So…how's your husband?" And she smiles and you *know* it's had the desired effect. You see it's not only brain surgeons and psychologists who work with the head. As for the hat brims, I've always said the larger the brim she wears the larger the life a woman wants to lead. I always used to make large brimmed hats for Amalia.

*(Living room in London. **AMALIA** stands in front of the mirror in a dressing gown and a large light blue wide brimmed hat. She tilts it one way, then another, looks desperate. Embarrassed as if caught looking at herself naked. **WOLFGANG** walks in.)*

AMALIA. I just thought I'd…

WOLFGANG. What are you doing Amalia?

AMALIA. I…I needed to remember how it felt. That's all.

WOLFGANG. I made that hat for you when we had

somewhere to go. Now you're wearing it to look at yourself.

AMALIA. *You* could look at me.

WOLFGANG. Yes, you're right. Actually you still look quite lovely in that hat. *(Stands back to admire her)* Yes, I'll look at you. No one else will in this country.

AMALIA. Wolfgang.

WOLFGANG. Yes.

AMALIA. *(Amalia tilts his chin upwards towards her face)* Let me see your eyes…Don't talk like that about the English.

WOLFGANG. I'm offending you?

AMALIA. They gave us visas.

WOLFGANG. They didn't want to.

AMALIA. They did though.

WOLFGANG. They shouldn't have.

AMALIA. You won't face it will you?

WOLFGANG. Stop.

AMALIA. Please try.

WOLFGANG. What should I try?

AMALIA. To accept it. They'd have deported her even if we'd stayed. She didn't *want* to leave. She didn't think she would die.

WOLFGANG. *(Shouts)* She's not dead!

AMALIA. *(Gently)* Face it, Wolfgang. No news is bad news. Horrible news. Accept it.

WOLFGANG. For what?

AMALIA. For you! For me. For us!

WOLFGANG. For you I came here. For you I get up and walk around the damned block ten times at five a.m. so your English friends won't intern me.

AMALIA. They won't intern you.

WOLFGANG. But why not? *(Sarcastic)* Let them drag me to their summer camp. This freedom of theirs is worse than prison.

AMALIA. You know Wolfgang, you don't have one ounce

of gratitude do you?...They're confused. They think we're Germans.

WOLFGANG. We are.

AMALIA. No, I mean real Germans.

WOLFGANG. We are *real* Germans. At least *I* am. What should I quote at you? Heine, Tucholsky, Kästner?

AMALIA. Wolfgang...Heine was a Jew. He just pretended he wasn't!

So you two have something in common. And Tucholsky's a Jew and Kästner's a Jew...

WOLFGANG. Germans.

AMALIA. *(Shouts)* Jews!! They had to get out too. No one singled you out. You're not so special. Don't you get it? They're out too. Just like us. Gone. Gone. Gone... and I'm sure their English is a damn sight better than yours by now.

(They are both quiet. He flops down in chair.)

AMALIA. If there'd been a child....

WOLFGANG. Then what?

AMALIA. You would've had to make an effort...for him.

WOLFGANG. Perhaps if you'd wanted one.

AMALIA. I didn't want...not there. You never said you minded.

WOLFGANG. No.

AMALIA. Perhaps we could still have one.

WOLFGANG. What? Here?

AMALIA. Why not?

WOLFGANG. It would be like planting an orchid in cement.

AMALIA. *(Amalia is silent for a moment)* It's three o'clock

WOLFGANG. And?

AMALIA. Well perhaps if I made you tea instead of coffee...A cup of tea at three o'clock you know...and a biscuit. *(Excited)* I got some in the rations today.

WOLFGANG. I'm not thirsty...and I don't want a *biscuit.* I don't want anything.

(Silence)

AMALIA. *(As if to herself)* Or should I light some candles? It's Friday.

I'm going to light some candles. *(Begins to get up)*

WOLFGANG. No Amalia. Please. *(Silence)*

AMALIA. Do you still love me?

*(**WOLFGANG** nods)*

AMALIA. You have to fight for it, Wolfgang. Drag it back up by its throat.

WOLFGANG. I'm fighting Amalia…I'm fighting.

*(A few moments silence. **AMALIA** still has her hat on. **WOLFGANG** looks at her)*

WOLFGANG. You wore it for our engagement and to the cabaret.

*(Back to cabaret. 1933. **CLAUDIA**, the blonde singer stands at a microphone in a tight fitting red dress and wide brimmed hat. **WOLFGANG** and **AMALIA** slip in. **CLAUDIA** begins to sing.)*

CLAUDIA. *(spoken:) Nimm dich in acht vor blonden frauen.*
(sung:) BE CAREFUL OF BLONDE WOMEN,
YOU MAY HAVE A WICKED SURPRISE
AT FIRST YOU MAY NOT NOTICE IT,
BUT DEEP INSIDE IT LIES.
YOU MAY LOVE THE WAY SHE LOOKS AND TALKS
BUT JUST BE CAREFUL OF THE FOX

(Applause. She bows. Takes her hat off and shows it off to the audience.)

CLAUDIA. In case you hadn't noticed I'm advertising "Claudia's"…my hat shop on Friedrichstrasse. I sell by day and sing by night…I know, I know, better than the other way round. *(Laughs)*…But seriously, there's a lovely hat in the front row, with an even lovelier face underneath. I didn't sell the hat, but I think I know the handsome man who made it.

WOLFGANG. *(*WOLFGANG *whispers to* **AMALIA***)* I know the shop.

AMALIA. You've been there?

WOLFGANG. She's bought from me. Our fathers knew each other. They fought together in the War.

AMALIA. She's beautiful isn't she?

WOLFGANG. Very German.

CLAUDIA. And I'm still selling to the most important heads in town.

BE CAREFUL OF BLONDE WOMEN,

You may have a wicked surprise!

(The Cabaret singer fades away as the scene dissolves and moves back to London with **WOLFGANG**, *lying on his bed listening to "Beware Of Blonde Women" on the gramophone.* **AMALIA** *is now sitting in front of her easel painting.* **AMALIA** *loses concentration, jumps up, comes over and scratches the needle across the record.)*

AMALIA. *(Shouts)* Enough! Do you hear me? Enough of this rubbish in my house. I've had enough. And get up Wolfgang. Open the curtains. This isn't like you.

(She leaves the room.)

WOLFGANG. There has to be a reason to get up.

AMALIA. Thank you. *(In the living room, back at her easel)*

WOLFGANG. *(Gets up slowly, goes into the living room, walks over to his wife)* Amalia, the way you are behaving, I worry you are losing your mind.

AMALIA. *(Doesn't look up)* You beat me to it.

WOLFGANG. Nonsense.

AMALIA. You should hear yourself. The things you call out in your nightmares *(Gentler tone)* You need help Wolfgang. We need help.

WOLFGANG. I'm not the one who paints everything in black.

AMALIA. At least I get it out.

(He turns away. Looks back.)

WOLFGANG. Amalia.

AMALIA. Yes.

WOLFGANG. I'm going back.

AMALIA. Back? *(Amalia looks up in disbelief and down again)*

WOLFGANG. To Berlin. As soon as this goddamned war is over. I'm going back.

AMALIA. *(Sarcastic)* Yes…yes, of course you are.

WOLFGANG. I'll take a few trips back. Try to build my clientele again so you and I can make a new life there Amalia. You won't admit it, but you'd be happier there too. *(Takes her face in his hands…then moves away)* I just can't sell here.

AMALIA. Nonsense, the English have heads that need hats too.

WOLFGANG. Yes, but their heads don't understand mine and my fingers won't create for them. It's as if…as if…I'm working with dried out clay…

AMALIA. You need to be more like them. Improve your grammar, your pronunciation. I'll help you with the verbs.

WOLFGANG. Your goddamned verbs…*(He mimics her)* I left, you left. We left.

*(**AMALIA** puts her face in her hands)*

WOLFGANG. I'm sorry Amalia.

AMALIA. It's just…not right. For us to even entertain the thought…

*(He crosses to a workbench in the living room, and begins to add the trimmings to a purple cloche. The spectre of Wolfgang's **MOTHER** appears in her orange beret and watches him at a distance.)*

AMALIA. *(Putting her coat on)* Wolfgang.

WOLFGANG. Yes.

AMALIA. That hat.

WOLFGANG. Yes.

AMALIA. Who's it for? Who's it for?

WOLFGANG. Frau Braunschweig. Do you remember her? Tiny woman. *(He gestures)...*I didn't finish it before we left...so I thought on my first trip back I'd...

AMALIA. Wolfgang, we've heard nothing of her.

WOLFGANG. Some people are not so good at keeping in touch.

AMALIA. It's been five years.

WOLFGANG. *(He is silent. He carries on working)* I hope her taste hasn't changed.

AMALIA. And that new beret you made for your Mother, Wolfgang. *(Speaks gently)* Throw it out. It's useless. You won't find her.

(He hammers the block with the cloche on it, carries on shaping the felt around the wooden hat block.)

AMALIA. I'm going out. *(Pause.)*

I'm going out, I said...to the Hyphen club...They're giving a talk...on cultural integration.

*(**WOLFGANG** almost spits. The **MOTHER** leaves. When she is gone, **WOLFGANG** calls after **AMALIA**.)*

WOLFGANG. You'll tell them all about Faust then......

(In a quieter voice) Be careful Amalia.

*(**WOLFGANG** pricks his finger with a needle by accident.)* Wolfgang Georg, you are going home. Berlin, I'm coming home.

*(**AMALIA** returns to pick up an umbrella.)*

AMALIA. Remember 1938?

You've got a short memory, Wolfgang Georg.

*(It is 1937. **WOLFGANG** sits in a train compartment surrounded by hatboxes. He reads the Berliner Tagesblatt. A man with a swastika on his sleeve walks in cap in hand...He is thin, straight-backed. He throws himself down with a sigh. Looks at Wolfgang with appreciation.)*

(A few moments silence.)

GERHARDT. Hat boxes, huh?

WOLFGANG. Yes, hat boxes.

GERHARDT. Buying or selling?

WOLFGANG. Selling.

GERHARDT. In Munich?

WOLFGANG. That's right.

GERHARDT. Interesting. You sell in Berlin also?

WOLFGANG. Of course. What would Berlin be without hats?

GERHARDT. What would hats be without Berlin?

(**WOLFGANG** *laughs.*)

GERHARDT. And who if I might ask are your customers?

WOLFGANG. Ah! Now that would be telling. But let's just say you will have seen my hats at the Philharmonic and at the Opera.

GERHARDT. Ah, the high society then. A handsome talented man selling to beautiful women! But no one seems to have much money for new hats these days. They take out their old ones *(Takes his cap off and dusts it)* and consider themselves dressed.

WOLFGANG. You seem to be in the know about my world.

GERHARDT. My wife…well it's a little complicated…but my wife has a small hat shop in Berlin.

WOLFGANG. A hat shop? *(Animated)* Not in the city centre?

GERHARDT. But of course it's bang in the centre. In the heart of it all on Friedrichstrasse.

WOLFGANG. Not Claudia's?

GERHARDT. Claudia's! Yes, yes. You know it?

WOLFGANG. Of course. What an extraordinary coincidence. She is a customer of mine…Our Fathers knew each other. They fought together in the war. I haven't heard from your wife in recent months though…I'm not exactly sure why…What a coincidence! I remember exactly the last time she bought from me. Two very dramatic scarlet hats with feathers. And some Parisian berets.

GERHARDT. Ah yes, I know the berets. Claudia sometimes wears one herself...And the scarlet hat she wore once on stage...A wonderful creation. She sings cabaret too you know.

WOLFGANG. Of course I know. I've heard her sing...I went to hear her at *Kaffee Kranzler*. She has a wonderful voice. She likes to sing the Dietrich numbers doesn't she?

GERHARDT. She does. Yes. *(He begins to sing, "Falling in Love Again" in English.)*
FALLING IN LOVE AGAIN, NEVER WANTED TO
*(**WOLFGANG** joins in)*
WHAT AM I TO DO?
CAN'T HELP IT.

(They laugh. Officer takes a small hipflask of whisky from his side pocket.)

GERHARDT. Can I offer you some? Gerhardt Müller.

WOLFGANG. *(Wolfgang nods acceptance.)* Wolfgang Georg.

GERHARDT. Listen, we still have a way to go. Would you mind showing me some of your hats?

WOLFGANG. Of course not. But the hatboxes are a little difficult to unpack.

GERHARDT. No problem, we'll do it together. I'm used to it. There must be order in the way we do this.

*(**WOLFGANG** kneels down on the floor next to his hatboxes. **GERHARDT** joins him. They untie the string around the boxes, unfold the top of the tissue paper. The officer peers into them.)*

GERHARDT. These are quality.

WOLFGANG. Why thank you.

GERHARDT. Where do you have them manufactured?

WOLFGANG. We don't. Hardly any at least. We design and make them ourselves.

GERHARDT. We?

WOLFGANG. My Mother and I.

GERHARDT. Really? How impressive. Truly impressive...And your Father lives off the two of you? *(He laughs.)*

WOLFGANG. No. He was killed, fighting for our country.

GERHARDT. I'm sorry. My father-in-law was badly injured. Too many good Germans were lost...Now come let's not talk of morbid things. Let's take a look at your hats. *(He lifts one up. A large hat with a huge feather. Strokes the feather)* This is for a confident woman. *(Picks out a velvet one with lace veil)* This is for a classy woman.

WOLFGANG. *(Picks up a satin hat)* This is for a sensual woman.

GERHARDT. Ach, ja! Ja ja. *(He picks out a cloche. Bell shaped hat)* This for a saucy woman. *(Gerhardt picks out a small brimmed hat)* For an uptight woman!

WOLFGANG. *(Picks out a mink)* A wealthy woman!

GERHARDT. *(Picks out a huge hat with a wide floppy brim. Turns it around on his finger. He laughs)* Ah, I know. This one's for a Jew. It hides her nose.

(Wolfgang's expression changes. Lights cross fade to the Cabaret Singer, singing "I Still Have A Suitcase In Berlin.")

CLAUDIA.

I STILL HAVE A SUITCASE IN BERLIN, THE ONE I KEEP MY FONDEST MEM'RIES IN

THE HAPPY DAYS THERE, THE MEM'RY STAYS THERE

STILL LOCKED INSIDE MY SUITCASE IN BERLIN.

I STILL HAVE A SUITCASE IN BERLIN

THE PLACE WHERE THOUGHTS OF TIME GONE BY BEGIN

I MUST RETURN THERE, FOR WHAT I YEARN THERE

TO LEAVE IT THERE ALONE NOW THAT WOULD BE A SIN.

TO LEAVE IT THERE ALONE.... I LONG FOR MY...

(spoken) Berlin.

Blackout

ACT TWO

(**CLAUDIA** *sings a refrain of "Falling in Love Again"*)

CLAUDIA.

FALLING IN LOVE AGAIN
NEVER WANTED TO
WHAT AM I TO DO?
CAN'T HELP IT.

MEN CLUSTER TO ME
LIKE MOTHS AROUND A FLAME
AND IF THEIR WINGS BURN
I KNOW I'M NOT TO BLAME

THAT'S WHY I'M
FALLING IN LOVE AGAIN
NEVER WANTED TO
WHAT AM I TO DO?
CAN'T HELP IT.

(*These three verses may be repeated.*)

(**WOLFGANG** *sits at the front of the stage. He is surrounded by brown leather hatboxes.*)

WOLFGANG. I wanted to prove to the Berliners I hadn't lost my touch, but the indigo velvet berets just didn't have quite the same panache when you had to have them manufactured in a godforsaken ghost town like Luton. I still made some of my hats myself of course, but at home there was the problem of the feather trim. Our living room became like a duck mortuary.

And then there was the money. Most of it, I borrowed from the manufacturer. His name was Marcus Marcus... Marcus Marcus. (*Said slowly*) As if he had to reiterate himself to get noticed.

An Anglicized Jew whose family had been there since the 17th century. (*In Marcus' voice and pronounces the W the English way:*) "Your accent Wolfgang. I can hardly understand a word you're saying. You don't belong in England. You should go home." (*Wolfgang:*) "As it happens, Mr. Marcus, you're right, but out of interest how long is it exactly before an immigrant gains the right to belong, huh?"

"Wolfgang, you are more German than the Germans. At least change your name to Bill or something a little more palatable.

Now, let's talk about the interest rate on this money. I'm not running a charity shop for refugees here."

(Wolfgang:) I wanted to ask him if he'd ever read *The Merchant of Venice.* I wanted to say, "How do you fancy leaving your beloved Luton from one day to the next and trying to conduct business in a foreign language?" But I kept quiet. I had too much at stake.

(WOLFGANG *walks over to a work- table. It is strewn with ribbons, feathers, velvet bands and half trimmed hats. He begins to trim a hat. Wagner plays in the background.*

He lifts a hand mirror to look at himself.)

"They're not even shadows, Amalia. I'm fine." "Are you sure you're not ill?" She must have asked me half a dozen times.

And it's like when someone asks you if you have a headache and you say "I'm fine, thank you," and five minutes later they ask you again. In the end you get a headache from their questions. So I started to get unnerved with Amalia's questions and she said she thought I was afraid to go back to Berlin. I mean, who would be afraid to go home?

Yes, I was tired, but there was something in my work that made me feel...that made me feel...so *free* really. But, I don't know...perhaps I did spend too much time with felts. Now when I think back...You know, I don't think I mentioned before that there's mercury in the fibers of the felt did I? They say it can make you a little crazy. The psychiatrists know about it...they say it can make you lose your mind...I don't know if it's connected...No, if I'm honest I couldn't say for sure how

I feel about that.

(Change of lighting. Change of tone. Remembers his enthusiasm at the idea of going back.)

I booked a room at a little hotel on *Fasanenstrasse*. The former concierge Max had known my family before the war...I mean my Mother. We'd set up some hat shows there. I wrote to him with a list and asked him to send out cards to my old customers. But I didn't get too *many* replies. I think I got...let me remember... I think I got...yes, I got one. So I asked Max to find out who...I mean...if anyone from the old lot was still selling hats and who was new on the scene. I prayed he'd do his homework and then in Spring of 1946 I left London for Berlin.

(1946. WOLFGANG stands surrounded by a brown leather trunk and hatboxes at the reception desk of the modest Savoy Hotel in Berlin.)

CONCIERGE. Herr Georg. How wonderful to see you back. Really I am so pleased. *(Grabs his hand and shakes it too strongly and for a long time.)*

WOLFGANG. Thank you.

CONCIERGE. You see our hotel survived the ravages of war. We're the only one in all of Berlin.

WOLFGANG. Oh. Really?

CONCIERGE. You must be tired from your journey...but you look...well, Sir.

WOLFGANG. Thank you.

CONCIERGE. This is our best suite. *(Whispers)* Actually I've given it to you for next to nothing. And the piano is through there. I remembered you played.

WOLFGANG. I used to. I haven't played since...

CONCIERGE. But the music never leaves you...you'll see. Oh, and we have had a few more replies to your invitations. Not as many as I would have liked though. The addresses have all changed...as you can imagine...and not everyone is still here...sadly...I mean...but it's a start. It will soon be back to business as normal. You'll see. You will have some new customers I'm sure.

WOLFGANG. I need them.

CONCIERGE. I understand. Oh...and...and your...family Herr Georg?

WOLFGANG. My wife is well...

CONCIERGE. *(Takes him to the door. Helps him in with the hatboxes. Goes to leave)* Herr Georg you'll need something to eat and to drink. I've arranged for some fruit and some of our special *Apfelstrudel. (Points in the direction of a tray)* You do like *Apfelstrudel?*

*(**WOLFGANG** nods.)*

CONCIERGE. Wonderful...wonderful. But you'll need something more substantial too. How about a nice Wiener Schnitzel? Some fried potatoes? A nice green salad with chives perhaps?

WOLFGANG. Maybe, yes...I'll have...No, I'll have a sandwich please. A cheese sandwich and a cup of tea.

CONCIERGE. A cheese and salami plate. We have wonderful salami.

WOLFGANG. A cheese sandwich please.

CONCIERGE. And some beer of course.

*(**WOLFGANG** has walked over to his suitcase which is close to the tray. He stares at the tray.)*

CONCIERGE. Did you want beer, Sir?

WOLFGANG. Oh, oh, no, just tea. Thank you.

CONCIERGE. Well that and the strudel should do the trick.

WOLFGANG. Thank you.

CONCIERGE. But I thought you said...

As you wish Herr Georg. Traveling is tiring, I'm sure...

(The Concierge starts to leave but...)

Herr Georg.

WOLFGANG. Yes.

CONCIERGE. I didn't know, you know. We didn't know.

(Lighting change. Hotel room doubles up as showroom. Wolfgang's hats are everywhere. The piano is almost covered. Draped with materials of every colour. **FRAU HENDEL** *stands by the door dressed in black.)*

WOLFGANG. Frau Hendel. How wonderful that you came. Please, let me take your coat.

(She makes no move to unbutton her coat.)

Now if I remember well, you liked everything from a plum red to a scarlet in hats didn't you?

FRAU HENDEL. Not anymore.

WOLFGANG. But why not? *(Upbeat)* Age shouldn't stop a love of colour.

FRAU HENDEL. I prefer black these days, but that's not why...

WOLFGANG. What, jet-black? With no break in the fabric? Look if it's a financial issue we can talk. I know times are tough. I...

FRAU HENDEL. It's not the money...

WOLFGANG. Ah, but you've come for a new look at least Frau Hendel.

A new look to celebrate a new start. A new Germany... now let me think...dark colours...hmmm...

(Wolfgang is trying to be more and more upbeat. **FRAU HENDEL** *is agitated.)*

Now this color would look wonderful in a pillbox hat I think. For ladies like you who love the Opera...if I remember correctly.

FRAU HENDEL. *(In a quiet voice)* The opera is completely destroyed, Wolfgang.

WOLFGANG. The Berlin Opera destroyed. That's unthinkable. I knew it had been damaged but I didn't know it was...I...

FRAU HENDEL. No, well why should you? You're in England now...I heard. That's good.

WOLFGANG. Yes,...for the moment. You know they have

such a sense of style, the English. I decided it would be the best place to make up my collection. There's a very salubrious small town where they manufacture... The Florence of Great Britain! It's called *(With a French accent)* Lu...ton.

And I'm partners with a true English gentleman.

A Mr. Marcus....So Frau Hendel maybe you want a practical hat?

FRAU HENDEL. No, Wolfgang – *(She looks down.)* That's not why I came.

WOLFGANG. A romantic hat then? Black can be romantic you know.

And we Berliners are romantic people are we not?

*(**FRAU HENDEL** just stares at him)*

The romance can't be dead, too.

FRAU HENDEL. *(Rummages in her bag)* I brought you these... these candlesticks. *(**WOLFGANG** stares at them)* And a Star of David necklace. Your mother asked me to hide them for her. I'm glad I can give them to you.

Do you remember the last time we all went to the Philharmonic together? Do you remember it Wolfgang?

(He nods.)

FRAU HENDEL. You and I and...I came...to pay my respects... I was told...I'm so sorry...I'm horrified that this happened...and to your Mother...She tried to be so strong without you...She...

WOLFGANG. I.....She thought I'd come back here one day. She said so.

FRAU HENDEL. *(Almost a whisper)* How did you find out?

WOLFGANG. *(He selects a hat and busies himself whilst talking to Frau Hendel)* A letter. We didn't hear for a long time... and then we did. I'm glad to see you yourself are so strong, Frau Hendel. No, no, please don't cry...it's too hard to fit a hat...It's too...hard...and please, don't blame yourself. You had nothing to do with any of it... you couldn't have...

FRAU HENDEL. I was here. I breathed in the air didn't I?... Didn't I?

(In tears she throws the hat to the ground and rushes to the door and leaves)

WOLFGANG. Frau Hendel...Please.

(Light fades on the scene.

After a few moments there is a knocking at the door of his suite. Lights up on **WOLFGANG** *staring at* **CLAUDIA.** *She wears a tailored coat, stilettos and an orange felt beret.* **WOLFGANG** *stands taken aback and stares.)*

CLAUDIA. Hello. Hello.

WOLFGANG. *(Hesitates)* Hello.

CLAUDIA. You remember me then?

*(**WOLFGANG** nods.)*

CLAUDIA. *(Laughs)* The way you're looking at me, I've obviously aged tremendously.

WOLFGANG. No...it was your hat...Your beret...I...

CLAUDIA. I wore it especially. I remembered I had bought it from you many years ago. *(Puts out her hand)* Herr Georg...how wonderful to see you. You are still so very handsome.

*(**WOLFGANG** kisses her hand. She walks in to the room past him towards the piano.)*

CLAUDIA. Ah! You've hidden the piano under your gorgeous materials. You were afraid I'd start playing.

WOLFGANG. No, no not at all. To be honest I had forgotten. Not that you were coming of course, but that you played the piano as well as sang. I had quite forgotten that.

CLAUDIA. I tried not to stop. I've been singing all the way through. Underground, for the soldiers, anywhere I could. Anything to make sure the vocal chords didn't atrophy.

These have not been easy times for us, Herr Georg.

WOLFGANG. No.

CLAUDIA. Pianos were hard to come by. They went up in flames with everything else. People used the legs for firewood.

WOLFGANG. And the nightclubs?

CLAUDIA. Bombed and burned. But not the Delphi! Right opposite this hotel. I sang there. I still do…No one pays me for it anymore. Gerhardt…my husband…well, we're not together anymore…but he never approved of me singing there. He thought the place was full of intellectuals and…well…unwanted people in hiding.

WOLFGANG. I see.

CLAUDIA. Herr Georg.

WOLFGANG. Yes.

CLAUDIA. *(She's referring to what he's been through)* What about you?

WOLFGANG. What about me?

CLAUDIA. Your hats. They're still gorgeous. You haven't lost your touch.

WOLFGANG. I would hope not.

CLAUDIA. Where were you?

WOLFGANG. In England. In London.

CLAUDIA. The rain capital of Europe.

WOLFGANG. *(He laughs)* Yes. They have more words for rain than letters of the alphabet. My wife wanted me to learn good English. But I've disappointed her. *(Beat)* I think a language either seeps into you or it doesn't. But I did learn all the synonyms for rain. I told her if you mastered the subject of rain you would never run out of conversation with the English. Over there it spits, it pours, it teems, it buckets, it drizzles. There are downpours and showers and heavens that open up! It even rains cats and dogs!

CLAUDIA. *(Walks around touching hats and materials)* It's awful that you stayed away for so long…Berlin needs your talent.

WOLFGANG. Thank you. We left…for obvious reasons.

CLAUDIA. Yes, yes, of course. *(Quizzically)* I never thought of
  you in that light though. Better not to…You know the
  women here never stopped wearing hats. They were
  bombed out of their homes. They were hungry. Many
  still are, but they still wear hats.

WOLFGANG. And the rest of the fashion industry?

CLAUDIA. It died….The important people are not here any
  longer. I…I take it you're coming back now then Herr
  Georg. For good, I mean.

WOLFGANG. Not just now. Not quite yet.

CLAUDIA. Your wife?

WOLFGANG. She's comfortable there. She's learnt excellent
  English. Made friends. Shown her paintings. Sold a
  couple even. My wife would have made a wonderful
  gipsy. She belongs everywhere. I admire her for that.

CLAUDIA. She didn't want to join you here?

WOLFGANG. She's busy.

CLAUDIA. The children?

WOLFGANG. We have none. And you?

CLAUDIA. No, no children. It's been rather lonely since I
  left Gerhardt.
  Not much lonelier than being with him I don't
  suppose.

WOLFGANG. I remember your husband. I met him once on
  a train from Berlin to Munich.

CLAUDIA. *(Astonished)* Really?

WOLFGANG. Yes. Seems like a lifetime ago. We fell into
  conversation. About my hat collection. Then we dis-
  covered the connection.

CLAUDIA. How extraordinary.

WOLFGANG. It was. He seemed fascinated by my hats.

CLAUDIA. *(Slightly disturbed by the recollection)* And by you, no
  doubt…You know what, at this precise moment I really
  don't feel like talking about him. I'm here with you to
  talk hats. Did I tell you I reopened recently?

WOLFGANG. No, you didn't. But that's wonderful. In the

same place? On Friedrichstrasse?

CLAUDIA. No.

WOLFGANG. Why not? It was a fabulous location.

CLAUDIA. Herr Georg, have you...?

WOLFGANG. Wolfgang.

CLAUDIA. Wolfgang, have you *seen* Berlin?

WOLFGANG. Not yet. I came in the dark last night. I haven't ventured out this morning. I've been too busy setting up my collection for you. I've heard, of course. But one never believes what one doesn't want to believe...

CLAUDIA. You should walk around. Your heart will break. Our poor architects, they toiled over plans for years.... and then this...this...devastation! Imagine how they must feel when they see their work burnt to nothing.

WOLFGANG. Yes...We met a Berlin architect in London at a supper party with my wife during the war....he was dismayed by the bombings.

CLAUDIA. A Berlin architect? In London during the war...? *(Pause.)* Oh. Oh, I see.

WOLFGANG. *(Looking around)* Anyway Claudia, have you seen anything you like yet?

CLAUDIA. I'm scared to start trying them on.

WOLFGANG. I'm delighted.

CLAUDIA. I have to be prudent though. I must be prudent. Must be prudent.

(Mantra fashion) Your hats are irresistible...just like your mother's.

(Lights cross fade on scene to the milliner's showroom, 1920's. Wolfgang's **MOTHER** *is fitting* **CLAUDIA** *with a beret as* **WOLFGANG** *watches.)*

MOTHER. Before you put them in your shop you need one of your own.

Dusty pink works perfectly on you. And you have such a hat face Claudia.

CLAUDIA. You have the hat face, Frau Georg. Those

cheekbones.

MOTHER. Oh? *(A little flustered. Touches her face)* My husband said he fell for my cheekbones before he fell for me.... Come here, Wolfgang. Just look at her. She's a raving beauty in this beret isn't she?

WOLFGANG. Yes, yes, I think I detect the raving beauty in her somewhere...

CLAUDIA. Why thank you, Sir. *(Looks in the mirror)* Well, I love it. When can I have it? When can I have it Frau Georg?

MOTHER. Tuesday. Anytime...

CLAUDIA. Tuesday. Tuesday. I'll have my pink beret. My rose beret. *(Breaks into "La Vie en Rose." Sings two lines of it in French as she moves towards the door)* Till Tuesday then.

MOTHER. *(To* **WOLFGANG***)* She's stunning *and* she's musical, Wolfgang.

WOLFGANG. Yes, Mother, and she has a large diamond on her finger.

MOTHER. Oh. I must have missed that...You never see what you don't want to see. *(Almost under her breath)* You'd be safe with her.

WOLFGANG. I felt sad for you, Mother. When you said how Father fell in love with your cheekbones. It's been so long. I'd be happy if you found someone.

MOTHER. Me? Find someone?

WOLFGANG. Well...Just some company.

MOTHER. I don't need company, Wolfgang. I have you. *(Exits.)*

(The lights fade, then come up again on **CLAUDIA &** **WOLFGANG** *in the hotel. Claudia plays Beethoven's "Pathetique.")*

CLAUDIA. So do you play?

WOLFGANG. I did. Before England. *(He gets closer to the piano. Clearly moved by the music.* **CLAUDIA** *turns round, smiles at him.)* I thought you used to just play cabaret music.

CLAUDIA. I play music.

(She pats the stool beside her. **WOLFGANG** *lifts up his hand as if to say no. He carries on listening. Then as if in a trance he walks over and sits next to her. The solo becomes a duet.)*

CLAUDIA. You see there are some things one never loses. It's just that they belong to a particular time or place. There are people who can only paint in the countryside.

WOLFGANG. Or write by the water.

CLAUDIA. Or think in the forest.

WOLFGANG. Or sell hats in Berlin.

CLAUDIA. Yes, yes. For God's sake let's get to hats.

WOLFGANG. Claudia. Do you go walking…in the forest… Near Nikolasee? *(Pronounced Nikolazay)* That's where we lived. My mother and I.

CLAUDIA. Close to there. By the Wannsee, I go.

WOLFGANG. The Wannsee? Wasn't that where the SS planned to…Yes, yes I've walked there, too. In another lifetime.

CLAUDIA. The countryside around there is so untouched. It's still as pure and thick with pine trees as ever. Do you remember the forest in the snow? Like the Goethe poem:
"Above all the treetops.
There's peace.
Between the pinecones…"

WOLFGANG. "There's not a breath to be felt."

CLAUDIA. "In the woods the tiny birds twitter."

WOLFGANG. "Wait a while, and you too will be at rest."

(Pause. A protracted moment of deep connection.)

CLAUDIA. These hats, they are for sale aren't they?

WOLFGANG. Look, I'm sorry I haven't even offered you a drink.

CLAUDIA. I could do with one. A whisky perhaps…or two.

WOLFGANG. Wonderful. The concierge got me a bottle

from somewhere. You'll buy more if you're tipsy.

CLAUDIA. I can hold my drink, Wolfgang.

WOLFGANG. We'll see about that...*In vino spenditas.*

CLAUDIA, WOLFGANG. Prost!

(*CLAUDIA laughs, gets up, picks a hat off a stand, puts it on, looks at herself in the mirror.*)

CLAUDIA. How's this?

WOLFGANG. Stylish, if I say so myself, but are they for you or the shop?

CLAUDIA. I *am* the shop. I don't see my own face when I try on hats. I see a million other women's faces in them.

WOLFGANG. I know what you mean. When I'm trimming them I see the faces of so many women I know in my mind. Women I knew.

CLAUDIA. You knew...in the biblical sense?

WOLFGANG. No, not "knew." Women I sold to. I've tried to find them. I...They were my friends...Anyway, you didn't come here for this.

(*They continue to drink whisky whilst she tries on the hats.*)

CLAUDIA. Give me a score out of ten for each one. Alright?

WOLFGANG. Alright.

CLAUDIA. This one?

WOLFGANG. Hmmm. A seven.

CLAUDIA. I won't buy it. And this?

WOLFGANG. An eight.

CLAUDIA. I'll have three. (*She twirls around*) And this?

WOLFGANG. A nine and a half!

CLAUDIA. Give me four. (*Looks at herself in the mirror. Sees him behind her. She points at him in the mirror.*) You, Wolfgang Georg are a true artist.

WOLFGANG. It's been a while since anyone has said that to me.

CLAUDIA. Your talent will break me.

WOLFGANG. Claudia. Would you mind? Could you sing something for me?...You don't have to. It was just an idea.

CLAUDIA. Another whisky! (*Reaches out*) It'll moisten my vocal chords. What shall I sing for you?

WOLFGANG. Didn't you sing Dietrich numbers?

CLAUDIA. Yes, I love her. She left, you know. Went to the U.S. (*Moves over to the piano*)

WOLFGANG. I heard. Of course.

CLAUDIA. So did Kurt Weil. That was a loss. I can't deny it.

(She sighs, then starts to play "You Do Something to Me." and begins to sing.)

YOU DO SOMETHING TO ME

SOMETHING THAT SIMPLY MYSTIFIES ME

TELL ME WHY SHOULD IT BE,

YOU HAVE THE POWER TO HYPNOTIZE–

CLAUDIA. Wolfgang...I'm sorry for what you've been through. Really, I am. But perhaps they just made themselves too obvious.

WOLFGANG. Obvious?

CLAUDIA. Not you. You were different. One barely knew. Besides *you* have class. And talent. And appeal. And I am going to buy every hat in the showroom.

WOLFGANG. (**WOLFGANG** *hesitates for a moment, then sits next to her at the piano*) You are the artist. Not me.

CLAUDIA. Thank you. Being here makes me feel...

*(She begins to kiss him there on the piano stool. The scene progresses from tender to passionate. They begin to undress, move across to the bedroom. The bed becomes the marital bed in London. **AMALIA** is lying there. Hears Wolfgang's key in the door. He drags hatboxes through the door.)*

AMALIA. (*Calls out*) Wolfgang, is that you? (**AMALIA** *sits up*) Wolfgang?

WOLFGANG. It's me. (*He walks in, stands in the doorway.*)

AMALIA. You're home.

WOLFGANG. I'm here. (**WOLFGANG** *looks at a harrowing unfinished painting.*)

You've been painting.

AMALIA. Yes, it's my sister.

WOLFGANG. Why do you do it to yourself?

AMALIA. It helps. *(She gets up. Helps him take off his coat)* You look tired, my love.

WOLFGANG. *(Wolfgang sinks down into a chair)* I sold Amalia. More than I could have dreamt of.

AMALIA. *(Amalia sits next to him on the arm of his chair. Takes his hand)* Tell me. Tell me.

WOLFGANG. 13 orders I had.

AMALIA. 13's not a lucky number.

WOLFGANG. For God's sake, Amalia. (*Gentle tone, takes both her hands*) I sold. I sold.

AMALIA. *(Amalia hugs him)* You're right. That's marvelous *(Pause)* So. Tell me.

WOLFGANG. What?

AMALIA. Berlin?

WOLFGANG. Don't ask.

AMALIA. Where did you go? Did you walk down *Unter den Linden?*

WOLFGANG. You can't get through. The Russians have put barbed wire right across it.

AMALIA. But it's ours.

WOLFGANG. Ours?

AMALIA. And the stores? Wertheim's, did you go? Did you bring me something ?

WOLFGANG. Wertheim's is gone Amalia.

AMALIA. *(Increasingly desperate)* But you went to drink something, didn't you? You sat in *Kaffee Kranzler.* You had *Milchkaffee* and *Apfelstrudel.*

WOLFGANG. No, Amalia I didn't have *Milchkaffee* and *Apfelstrudel.* And there is no *Kaffee Kranzler* any more.

AMALIA. And the trees Wolfie? Is the almond blossom out yet?

WOLFGANG. There are no trees anymore.

AMALIA. No trees? Don't be ridiculous.

WOLFGANG. We bombed them.

AMALIA. We?

WOLFGANG. Your British friends.

One evening early I walked down Eislebener Strasse. My hotel and the cabaret opposite it, the Delphi... you remember it...? They were the only buildings still standing on the street. The others had been ravaged. There were children kicking pieces of brick around in these huge empty spaces. I walked to the Kempinski Hotel. The outdoor café on the corner was gone but there was this old man standing there drinking from a china cup. He saw me staring, "Sir, sir, come over here a moment. I have a story to tell you...I drank my coffee here every morning for fifty years with my wife. The bombs got her...the British you know, so now I come to this street corner every morning and drink coffee in memory of her...it helps me keep her face in my mind...And you, Sir, you look like a lucky man. No one you loved taken by the bombs I hope?" I walked for miles, Amalia. My shoes were filthy from the rubble and...and it was all so...vulnerable...and bare.

But the sky was getting red...and the light was marvelous. That's one thing they couldn't bomb, Amalia... the Berlin light...You remember it? (**AMALIA** *nods, engrossed*)

I walked East. I wanted to see the Philharmonic before it got dark. I thought I was walking in the wrong direction. You remember you could see it from miles away? I thought I had got lost in my own city. And then I heard the music. Rising up from somewhere. It was Mahler. His Seventh. I followed the sound...and then I saw them...they were standing there in the open air...rehearsing in the dried out grass with their suits and ties on. Playing to the sky as though it were a full house. The sound was beautiful but thin. There weren't enough musicians. There were gaps in the rows. I stood there for ages and listened to them.

(Mahler plays in the background. **AMALIA** *leads him into the bedroom. They lie there for a while next to each other.)*

AMALIA. Wolfgang.

WOLFGANG. Yes.

AMALIA. We haven't for ages.

WOLFGANG. I know.

AMALIA. Do you want to?

WOLFGANG. I don't know. I can't…I…

AMALIA. Perhaps we need some help.

WOLFGANG. Oh nonsense.

AMALIA. We used to. Often. Or have you forgotten?

WOLFGANG. Of course I haven't forgotten.

AMALIA. We used to. Remember. *(She laughs, then grows subdued.)* Back there.

WOLFGANG. I know.

AMALIA. Maybe if we went away for a few days. I mean you sold hats. You said you sold.

WOLFGANG. I did. She bought some of almost every model for her shop. She used to have her place on Friedrichstrasse. You remember, Amalia? Claudia, the woman who sang at *Kaffee Kranzler* the night you wore your black hat.

AMALIA. Yes, yes, I remember vaguely.

WOLFGANG. She came in and she saw there was a piano in the room and she played and then….then…she made me play.

AMALIA. *(Sits up, shakes him)* You played Wolfy, you played the piano. I don't believe it.

WOLFGANG. It's true. I played a little.

AMALIA. Come then. Come. Play a little for me, Wolfy. Please.

WOLFGANG. I can't Amalia. I'm sorry, I can't.

AMALIA. But you said you could…you did…

WOLFGANG. I did…there.

AMALIA. Perhaps you dreamt it.

AMALIA. Wolfy?

WOLFGANG. Yes.

AMALIA. I…I don't like it when you're not here.

WOLFGANG. You're afraid?

AMALIA. I have too much time to think.

WOLFGANG. I don't want you to be afraid.

AMALIA. I won't be anymore. You're here. *(She begins to kiss him, then stops.)* It's no good is it, Wolfgang?

WOLFGANG. I don't know what to say… I

AMALIA. I'm worried…I…

WOLFGANG. Shhhh…Amalia…shh…come here, I'll hold you. Let's get some sleep. Sleep. Get some sleep.

(They hold each other tightly to a refrain of "Falling In Love Again" as the light very slowly fades away.

From the darkness, the sound of **WOLFGANG** *muttering in his sleep can be heard, building to a crescendo.)*

WOLFGANG. You've forgotten it! You've forgotten it! Here. Don't leave it. Mother, Mother, it will keep you warm. Never go out without your hat. Here, take it. No, No, Please, please. Mother…Take it with you. This one. Take it…Here…Take it…Take it…Take it!!!

(She wakes him.)

AMALIA. Wolfgang, I can't bear to see you like this. These nightmares are impossible. It's been like this since Berlin.

WOLFGANG. It's nothing. It's not serious.

AMALIA. They wake me up, Wolfgang. You scream things out.

WOLFGANG. Oh yes? *(Sarcastic)* What sort of things?

AMALIA. About your mother! You keep screaming for your

Mother.

WOLFGANG. Stop for God's sake stop, Amalia. This is nonsense.

(He begins to dress.)

AMALIA. It's the middle of the night. You need some sleep.

WOLFGANG. I don't want to sleep. It's useless.

AMALIA. Wolfy, I've found someone who can help us. Rolph Feder is his name. He's one of us.

WOLFGANG. Are you talking about the Jewish thing again?

AMALIA. He'll understand. He'll help you deal with this love affair *(tiniest of pauses)* with Germany. *(The intention is to show that* **AMALIA** *believes he's having a love affair with Germany.)*

WOLFGANG. I don't have time. I have to get back to Berlin next week. I have to deliver the orders. People are walking around with bare heads because of me.

AMALIA. *(Puts her hands on his shoulders)* Wolfgang, we…You and I are more important than bare German heads.

WOLFGANG. I don't need a psychiatrist.

AMALIA. I'm begging you, Wolfgang.

WOLFGANG. You could go, Amalia. If you feel the need! I can't. Perhaps after Germany.

(Back to Berlin. In the hotel room. The place is full of hats.)

CLAUDIA. Your hats Wolfgang Georg, belong in my shop. They are selling like Bratwurst on the street corner.

WOLFGANG. Ah! Bratwurst, don't remind me. *(Sniffs, remembering)* My Mother…my Mother used to take me when I was small to get Bratwurst on Sevignyplatz. I can still see myself standing on tiptoe to pay the man who grilled the sausages. His front teeth were missing. *(Smiles.)*

CLAUDIA. They still sell them you know. There's a man on Friedrichstrasse. He sold his Bratwurst while the bombs fell around him…he didn't leave till he ran out of sausage meat.

WOLFGANG. And then he came back?

CLAUDIA. He did. It's as if he ignored the war. We could go. Not just yet though. I want...I want to be with you a little.

WOLFGANG. Yes.

CLAUDIA. I've been thinking about you.

WOLFGANG. And I you.

CLAUDIA. A woman came in and tried the indigo blue hat...the one with the big, floppy brim. One of your old styles I think. She said, "this designer is so special" and I said "Yes, yes he's very special."

WOLFGANG. Thank you. *(Moves closer to her)* So, how have you been Claudia?

CLAUDIA. It's been pretty nightmarish...I want an official divorce from Gerhardt. Not that I need it, but the piece of paper would help me move on. But who knows where the man's hiding himself now. Brazil, Argentina...somewhere exotic I would imagine.

But you know, he never did want this divorce. He wanted to keep up appearances...Oh, he's always known he's had no choice of course. I know too much about him.

WOLFGANG. *(Hopeful)* So that's why you left him then? Because of what you know? Because of what he did?

CLAUDIA. Yes.

WOLFGANG. So, so what was it? What did he do? *(Puts his hand up as if to stop her)* No, I don't...

CLAUDIA. He had an affair...with a man. He has long preferred men. That part of my life was non-existent. It wouldn't matter if it leaked out now...He's in a different kind of danger, but before...if they had known... Oh God, if the SS had known.

WOLFGANG. *(Disappointed)* I see. That was it.

CLAUDIA. Wolfgang. Enough of this blackness. *(Reaches out to him)* I've missed you. I have no right, but I've been lonely without you.

WOLFGANG. I have to admit, I...I can't stop thinking about you either.

CLAUDIA. No, I mean really. I've missed you as if I knew you. I sang something that made me think of you last week.

(Begins to sing, "Here beneath the linden," which his Mother had sung to him. She sings the first verse in English unaccompanied.)

HERE BENEATH THE LINDEN THE OLD TREES BLOOM AGAIN

NOTHING CAN EVER CHANGE WHEN BERLIN IS STILL BERLIN

WHEN YOU CAN TRUST NO OTHER MY TRUST IS EVERGREEN

YOU ARE MY OLDEST LOVER: BERLIN IS STILL BERLIN

You need to come back here Wolfgang. Not just these jaunts to sell. You need to come home. You belong to this place. You belong....*(She starts to kiss him)* To the music...to the people...to me. So...Will you come back?

WOLFGANG. Perhaps soon...I...

CLAUDIA. You will come back won't you, Wolfgang? Tell me you'll come back.

WOLFGANG. I need to. I...need to...I'm not sure how to...I

*(In London. **WOLFGANG** walks through the door. **AMALIA** throws her arms around his neck. She is dressed in higher heels than usual. Her dress reveals her cleavage. **WOLFGANG** holds her a little stiffly. Looks past her over her shoulder as she speaks)*

AMALIA. I missed you so much.

WOLFGANG. That's nice, Amalia. That's nice...Smells good.

AMALIA. *(Laughs)* Me or the cooking?

*(**WOLFGANG** pats her back and extricates himself.)*

WOLFGANG. What is it? What have you made?

AMALIA. Meatballs...the way your Mother taught me. Your favorite.

WOLFGANG. Why those all of a sudden?

AMALIA. My mind was racing while you were away. We need to make more of an effort. I want my old Wolfgang back.

(She busies herself with laying the table. He takes his coat and hat off. He notices two lit Sabbath candles on the sideboard. Starts but says nothing.)

WOLFGANG. The meatballs smell delicious...I'll go and wash my hands.

AMALIA. *(She calls after him)* I've been thinking about what we discussed before you left...

WOLFGANG. What was that?

AMALIA. We'll talk about it over dinner.

WOLFGANG. I see you put the linen serviettes out.

AMALIA. I thought if I brought a little of Berlin here, it might help.

WOLFGANG. Hmm.

AMALIA. You know, if I say so myself, I think this food is going to be almost as good as your Mother's. Are you not hungry?

WOLFGANG. Not so much, but I feel guilty...all this effort for me.

AMALIA. I was thinking. You remember I told you about Doctor Feder.

WOLFGANG. Doctor Feder?

AMALIA. The psychiatrist.

WOLFGANG. You wanted a nice evening Amalia.

AMALIA. No time is the right time. You promised you'd consider it.

WOLFGANG. I considered it.

AMALIA. What about me, Wolfgang? Do you ever think I might be suffering too?

WOLFGANG. *(He looks up)* Yes.

AMALIA. There's no stigma you know. Your Mother went.

WOLFGANG. *(Almost laughs)* Yes, oh yes she did. She said her analyst saved her life.

I mean…she used to say *(He counts four items on his fingers)* "My son, my hats, my cooking, and Dr. Bachmann make it all worthwhile."

(The lighting changes. Wolfgang's MOTHER walks in with an Apple Strudel. She sits at the table with WOLFGANG and AMALIA.)

MOTHER. You'll have to imagine the second helping of *apfelstrudel.* There wasn't enough. But… I did find the apples….

WOLFGANG. You're quite something Mother.

AMALIA. *(Putting her fork down)* I'll never be able to cook for him like you do.

MOTHER. It doesn't matter, Amalia. Just love him as much as I do. *(She bows her head and tries to compose herself)* I'm sorry, I promised myself I wouldn't get emotional. Dr. Bachmann and I have practiced this a thousand times.

AMALIA. Irmgart, won't you change your mind?

WOLFGANG. We'll get you a visa, Mother.

MOTHER. Wolfy, no, we've been through this too often.

AMALIA. There's time Irmgart.

MOTHER. No, no I've made my decision. Please don't ask me again. I would be nothing outside Berlin. You're still young enough. You'll make a good life there…or perhaps you'll come back when all this madness has blown over. That's it. That's something to look forward to. You'll come back.

WOLFGANG. Amalia, I think…I think this is not a good idea. I think we should stay with Mother.

MOTHER. Wolfgang, I'll lose my temper. Now go. You're not a child. Get your coats on and leave. I have work to do. *(Looks at her watch.)*

(AMALIA gets up, puts on her hat and coat. WOLFGANG

stays sitting.)

AMALIA. I'll give you two a few minutes together.

(Goes to her mother-in-law. They embrace.)

Thank you, thank you. Goodbye, Irmgart...Goodbye. Wolfgang, I'll wait at the corner. I'll sit on the bench. It's nice outside. The almond blossom....

(She rushes offstage fighting back tears)

WOLFGANG. Mother, I.....

MOTHER. Don't start Wolfgang. You were like this as a boy. You'd get a bee in your bonnet and you'd nag and nag.

WOLFGANG. I don't know why I'm doing this Mother.

MOTHER. Because you owe it your wife...and to yourself. And to me....you think I taught you to make the most beautiful hats in the world to see your business dwindle to nothing. You'll teach the English a thing or two about style.

WOLFGANG. Mother, how will you manage?

MOTHER. You underestimate your Mother.

WOLFGANG. No, no I never underestimate you.

*(**MOTHER** helps him on with his hat and coat. They hug. She pushes him towards the door. **AMALIA** calls to him as if telling him to hurry and his **MOTHER** calls to him as if to say goodbye at almost the same time. His Mother's call is almost an echo.)*

AMALIA. Wolfgang.

MOTHER. Wolfgang.

AMALIA. Wolfgang.

MOTHER. Wolfgang. Wolfgang!

*(**MOTHER** exits. Lighting changes. **AMALIA** and **WOLFGANG** back in London.)*

AMALIA. *(Gentle)* Wolfgang. Wolfgang you're not listening to me...Wolfgang.

WOLFGANG. *(Distracted)* Yes.

AMALIA. I need you to hear what I'm saying to you, Wolfy!

WOLFGANG. What is it, Amalia?

AMALIA. You're somewhere else.

WOLFGANG. Walking in the forest with Mother. At the Wansee.

AMALIA. The Wansee. You want to go walking where the SS planned to wipe us out? You're crazy. Wolfgang, if your mother could go and talk to someone, you can….just once…please…. Wolfgang, say something…. Can I at least make an appointment for us?

(**WOLFGANG** *speaks as if to a psychiatrist.*)

WOLFGANG. Not everyone doctor can be as strong about having their roots ripped out from under them as my wife. Some of us can no longer find any hat that fits. In the dead of Winter we feel the skin of our scalps grow red and raw. And it hurts Doctor. It's *Heim Weh…* *(Pronounced Himevay)* quite literally "pain for home." It grips you and drags you back there by the skin of your throat *(His hand on his own throat)* and you are so drawn to them and you feel so guilty for it all at once. And so you leave again and you come back here…to this place and you struggle to be one of "*them.*" And you feel so…so utterly alone and you don't even really know who you are anymore. How can you, when you can't see yourself reflected in anybody's eyes?

(Lighting change. Showroom cum hotel room in Berlin. **CLAUDIA** *is dressing for the cabaret.)*

CLAUDIA. I want you with me at the cabaret.

WOLFGANG. I'm not sure I can. I'd love to hear you sing, but there'll be people…a room full of people who…

CLAUDIA. Yes, a room full of music lovers like us. Like us, Wolfgang. *(goes up to him…smoothes his brow)* These frown lines. You don't need them when you're with me. You're just worried that all the men will fall in love with me.

WOLFGANG. That wouldn't be difficult at all. To fall in love with you. To fall totally in love with you.

CLAUDIA. I like hearing you say that.

WOLFGANG. Look, I do want to come with you, Claudia… it's just…

CLAUDIA: You'll be anonymous there, Wolfgang. Look, in name I'm still married too and I don't care. Anyway we don't need to talk to anyone. You'll just listen to me sing. I still don't know enough about your life…

WOLFGANG. What's there to know? I'm a milliner, a plain old hat salesman according to the English and you are an extraordinarily alluring cabaret singer–

CLAUDIA. No, Wolfgang. That's not enough. We both know that. I need to understand. *(Pause.)*
It can't be easy for you to be torn this way…between loyalty to her and…this. I want to know.

WOLFGANG. I think about you all the time. Obsessively really. How do I explain…how?

CLAUDIA. By talking to me…Oh I don't mean the "historical," stuff that's bound to make you feel awkward. But the part of your emotional life that *does* matter. We should talk about it…

WOLFGANG. Yes.

CLAUDIA. *(Shakes her head)* If anyone had told me, that I'd be here, like this, with you. That I'd feel this for you… for a Je-(*pronounces the very beginning of the word "Jew."*)
But I do understand you, you know.
I found a poem that reminded me of you the other day. It's a Heine.
I had to hide the book after '33.

CLAUDIA. *(reciting:)* "When I find myself in your arms,
Calmed by your kisses,
Then please don't talk to me of Germany,
I have my reasons,"

CLAUDIA & WOLFGANG. "I simply can't take it.

WOLFGANG. I had a homeland that kissed me
In German, that spoke to me in German

In German, 'I Love You" sounded like a
Dream. It was a dream." *(Wolfgang's quasi recognition of the impossibility of the situation)*

*(**CLAUDIA** puts "La Vie en Rose" on the gramophone and crosses to him.)*

CLAUDIA. Wolfgang.

WOLFGANG. Yes?

CLAUDIA. Dance with me.

(He stands up and there begins an intimate slow dance on stage.)

*(Lights cross fade on the scene to **WOLFGANG** at his worktable in London. Behind him are shelves containing an assortment of wooden blocks for hat shapes. Wolfgang's **MOTHER** is omnipresent.)*

AMALIA. Wolfgang.

WOLFGANG. *(Focusing on choosing a material)* Yes.

AMALIA. Wolfgang, I've been thinking. Perhaps you should look into some sort of memorial stone for your Mother. I think it's time.

WOLFGANG: *(He picks out a basic felt hat model, dusts it off)* I haven't really talked about the procedure for making a hat before, have I? You need to have a design in your mind. If you go for a felt or a straw basic, then you have to choose the block to shape it on. When I was small choosing a block from my Mother's shelves was as exciting as choosing a flavor in the ice cream shop.

AMALIA. Wolfgang, we could pick out the stone together. Something beautiful. We could put purple pansies around it. She loved pansies didn't she? Late Spring is the right time to do it.

WOLFGANG. You've always got the season in mind when you choose a hat design. You have to imagine blistering heat when you're still numb with cold.
And then you'll press the felt hard over the block. You'll push and you'll shape. As though you were sculpting.

AMALIA. I thought you might choose a piece of Goethe or some Heine for her tombstone. She loved Heine didn't she? Didn't she, Wolfgang?

WOLFGANG. And you have to cut the model around the edges and then tie it tight around the block with string. Tie and pull and pull.

(Lights dim to show he is working into the early hours.)

WOLFGANG. And you have to nail it at the edges to get the right shape. And sometimes you have to bang the felt into the block to get the creases out. Hard, really hard. Knock the nonsense out of it.

AMALIA. *(From the doorway)* It would have been her Birthday in May. I thought you might want to do it in time for that. And I'll come back with you for the unveiling Wolfgang. I'm ready to come back to Berlin for you.

WOLFGANG. You have to make sure all the creases are banged in to the block…Like this, like this, like this. Make it look right. Like this, this. *(Hammers aggressively)* Get the creases out. You have to make it look rightyou have to…you have to…

*(His voice breaks. He puts his head on the table. **AMALIA** comes over to console him. Lights fade.*

*Music plays as **CLAUDIA** and **WOLFGANG** walk into the cabaret in Berlin together. **CLAUDIA** is in a gold sequined dress. She stops and straightens his tie.)*

He takes her arm. They are approaching a table where, by coincidence two of her male friends are sitting. They get up to greet her)

PAUL. Claudia.

CLAUDIA. What a surprise!

PAUL. How wonderful.

HEINZ. You look…

PAUL. Ravishing.

CLAUDIA. Heinz, Paul, this is my friend Wolfgang Georg.

HEINZ. Delighted to meet you.

PAUL. A pleasure.

WOLFGANG. Pleased to meet you too.

PAUL. Do you mind if we join you?

CLAUDIA. Please do, of course.

> (**WOLFGANG** *sits down. Background music*)

PAUL. Look what I have here. A bottle. *(Puts one on the table)*

HEINZ. Two…And I'm popping first.

CLAUDIA. Where on earth did you get these from?

PAUL. Let's just say there's a GI who's crazy for my sister.

CLAUDIA. Let's drink to Wolfgang…a true artist, a talented fellow musician, and the best of German milliners. Without him my head would be bare.

HEINZ. And your eyes would have distinctly less sparkle.

PAUL. To Wolfgang.

HEINZ. To new acquaintances.

PAUL. Prost!

HEINZ, WOLFGANG, CLAUDIA. Prost!

CLAUDIA. *(Leaving the table leans over to* **PAUL***)* I better go and get ready. You'll look after him won't you?

PAUL. Go, Claudia. Go. *(Ushers her away)* We'll take excellent care of him. Any friend of yours is a friend of ours.

HEINZ. *(As* **CLAUDIA** *walks over and goes offstage)* So, Wolfgang, are you a Berliner?

WOLFGANG. Yes, yes, I was born in Berlin.

HEINZ. And stayed here all the way through?

WOLFGANG. No, well yes, until the last few years.

PAUL. Ah, where were you?

WOLFGANG. I've been…away from home.

PAUL. Ah, one of those who doesn't talk about the past… we're all in the same boat…So, Claudia says you're a musician.

WOLFGANG. An amateur one, I would say. An amateur pianist. And you?

PAUL. I'm a violinist.

WOLFGANG. With an orchestra?

PAUL. A quintet actually...and solo from time to time. And Heinz here, he's a superb cellist.

HEINZ: Paul, you exaggerate. I'm not in the same league as you. I didn't quite make their grade. *(Referring to the SS's choice of music.)*

PAUL. No, no, it's true. I always loved playing in a quintet with you.

WOLFGANG. Maybe you could start a new one.

PAUL. Start what?

WOLFGANG. An quintet...a new Berlin Quintet...

HEINZ. What a marvelous idea. We'll get some more strings. And you'll be our pianist Wolfgang.

WOLFGANG: I don't think I'm quite up to that.

PAUL. Not what we just heard. Claudia says you're a talent. I think it's a superb idea. Let's drink to it.

HEINZ. Prost.

PAUL. Prost...

WOLFGANG. Prost.

(They clink glasses.)

WOLFGANG. Were you able to play these last few years?

PAUL. Yes. Private parties, official gatherings.

WOLFGANG. *(Half laughs)* Well, if the music's in you, you have to play...I think.. I

HEINZ. Now that's the truth. Paul was the lucky one. They wanted him through it all. Him, Beethoven, and Wagner.

WOLFGANG. Ah, Wagner?

PAUL. Of course. Wagner. Prost!

HEINZ. Prost!

*(**WOLFGANG** pours himself some more drink.)*

*(**HEINZ** and **PAUL** clink glasses. Lift their glasses to clink with Wolfgang's but he is drinking and doesn't move his*

glass towards theirs)

HEINZ. So how do you feel about post-war Berlin?

WOLFGANG. *(Obvious he has to make a big effort to make small talk)* It's er, well the…um…devastation is…it's really…

HEINZ. Shocking isn't it? Ghastly, with the potential to be marvelous again.

PAUL. Indeed!

HEINZ. It's this feeling of freedom which is so goddamned wonderful. Don't you think? I'm so delighted not to be stuck in an airless office any more.

WOLFGANG. Ah…You were a clerk?

HEINZ. Up the road here actually, in the Ministry. They had to find something to do with me. I wasn't fit for much else. *(Taps his injured leg)*

WOLFGANG. So what were you doing?

HEINZ. Inventories. You know.

WOLFGANG. Inventories?

HEINZ. Lists of items. Nothing of major consequence. Nothing too meaningful to anyone I don't imagine. And I didn't get much out of it

PAUL. Ah, but show him what you did get, Heinz. Show him the watch.

*(**HEINZ** puts up his hand as if to say "no" and shushes **PAUL**.)*

PAUL. Oh, go on, show him. No one's coming back to claim it.

*(**HEINZ** lifts his shirt sleeve and shows **WOLFGANG** his watch.)*

HEINZ. From under heaps of them. She's a goddamned beauty isn't she? Here. Feel the weight of her.

*(The spectre of Wolfgang's **MOTHER** starts to appear. **WOLFGANG** sits immobilized . He begins to cough. **PAUL** comes round and bangs him on the back. **WOLFGANG** pushes him off slightly too roughly, reaches for his glass again.)*

CLAUDIA. *(As she takes the microphone:)* Ladies and Gentle-
men. It's hugely exciting for me to be back here. A
first since this cabaret has been reopened. Two people
have helped me in my choice of this song. The first is
as always Marlene Dietrich who inspires me endlessly.
The second is a very good friend of mine, sitting right
over there. (*Points towards* **WOLFGANG**) So tonight for
Marlene and for Wolfgang and for all of you…

(**CLAUDIA** *sings a Cabaret Montage*)

CLAUDIA.

I STILL HAVE A SUITCASE IN BERLIN
THE ONE I KEEP MY FONDEST MEMORIES IN
THE MEN I KNEW THERE
THE THINGS I'D DO THERE
STILL LOCKED INSIDE MY SUITCASE IN BERLIN

FALLING IN LOVE AGAIN
NEVER WANTED TO,
WHAT I AM TO DO
CAN'T HELP IT
And I can't explain it, but…
YOU DO SOMETHING TO ME
SOMETHING THAT SIMPLY MYSTIF—

IT HAD TO BE YOU
IT HAD TO BE YOU
I WANDERED AROUND
AND FINALLY FOUND
SOMEBODY WHO

MOTHER ,CAN YOU NOW FORGIVE ME
MOTHER, DOES HURT STILL REMAIN
MOTHER, CAN YOU NOW FORGIVE ME
FOR CAUSING YOU SUCH –

YOU MAY LOVE THE WAY SHE LOOKS AND TALKS
BUT JUST BE CAREFUL OF THE FOX
BE CAREFUL OF BLONDE WOMEN
YOU MAY HAVE A WICKED SURPRISE!

(The applause is enthusiastic. **WOLFGANG** *barely claps.*

CLAUDIA *goes over to* WOLFGANG *and her friends. The table is by the window. Everyone is a little drunk.)*

PAUL. You were astonishing, Claudia.

HEINZ. Fabulous, Claudia, out of this world.

CLAUDIA. And you ,Wolfgang, how did you like it? How was I?

WOLFGANG. *(Distracted)* Very good.

CLAUDIA. It was all for you my darling.

PAUL. It's marvelous being back here again.

HEINZ. It's been too long, far too long.

(Absentmindedly pours her a drink. It spills over the side.)

PAUL. Come on, drink up, drink up. *(Fills the glasses)* Prost, prost, prost.

(They all clink glasses, but WOLFGANG *appears troubled.)*

To a new Berlin!

PAUL, HEINZ, CLAUDIA. A new Berlin!

PAUL. To Summer nights in Berlin. To romance.

HEINZ. To romance! Let's drink to romance…to the stars and the moon. Look out there people. Look out. A full moon. Which one of us is going to go mad then?

(They laugh, looking outside.)

PAUL. I will be sent mad by the joy of your company.

CLAUDIA. I will be sent mad with the beauty of the evening.

PAUL. I will be sent mad by the talent of our singer

CLAUDIA. God, look. Look, those rats out there look mad. Must be the full moon. Look at them….scurry, scurry in the gutter…look…just like the *Jews* being rounded up.

HEINZ. *(laughing)* The Jews!

(Lights fade on the trio laughing hysterically.)

(The lights rise on **WOLFGANG** *in the same position but now back at the hotel.* **CLAUDIA** *is changing unseen in the bathroom.)*

CLAUDIA. *(Calls out, her voice a little slurred)* I'm changing for you sweetheart. It was fabulous tonight, just fabulous that you were there. In...tox...ic...ating. I'm soooo happy. They seemed to love me. Like the old times.

(She begins to hum the tune of "Mutter, hast Du mir vergeben... Mother have you forgiven me?" Then comes out of the bathroom in a nightdress.)

CLAUDIA. Wolfgang, Wolfgang, I don't hear you clapping. You're sooo quiet, Wolfgang....*(She comes up and teases him, takes his hands and claps them together)* I want to hear your applause darling. Are we a little drunk then?

WOLFGANG. Drunk? Yes...no...not quite drunk.

CLAUDIA. Let's have some more?

(She dims the lights and pours two glasses of Champagne. They drink. She begins to kiss and touch him... He responds at first.)

CLAUDIA. Wolfgang, my love.

WOLFGANG. Claudia... *(He touches her face, then moves his hands away conflicted)*

CLAUDIA. Yes.

WOLFGANG. What was that you said?

CLAUDIA. I said "Wolfgang my love." My love, I said, my love.

WOLFGANG. No, before, in the cabaret...tell me...what did you say?

CLAUDIA. I said it was all for you. For you...and...for... Marlene.

WOLFGANG. Not that. That's not what I'm talking about.

CLAUDIA. Sshhh! This...is not...the time...for talking.

(She begins to kiss him again between words. Again he pulls back)

WOLFGANG. No, no, I need....to know...before...by the

window?

CLAUDIA. Shhhh. Wolfgang. Shhhhh.....

WOLFGANG. What...did you say?

CLAUDIA. When? What are you talking about?

WOLFGANG. What did you see...in the full moon? In the gutter?

CLAUDIA. The gutter? Oh, the rats? In the light of the full moon....The full blue moon.

(She begins singing, "Blue Moon" as the spectre of Wolfgang's MOTHER *appears.)*

*(*WOLFGANG *puts his hand over* CLAUDIA*'s mouth as she sings. Her words are muffled)*

WOLFGANG. Stop*!* About the rats, what did you say about the rats? *(He lets go.)*

CLAUDIA. *(Startled)* The rats?....in the gutter...in the moonlight.

WOLFGANG. And they looked like what? What were the rats like? Say it. Go on. Say it.

CLAUDIA. *(Spits it out)* The Jews....The Jews rounded up.

*(*WOLFGANG *walks away from her. She follows him. They appear, at first to be making love.)*

WOLFGANG. The Jews like the rats, huh? That's it... that'swhat you said is it? The rats like the Jews...yes? yes? Yes? Do we...my love? We look like the rats? That's what you think...of us? *(She begins to choke)* The rats like us. We...look...like...rats...

*(*WOLFGANG *loses control of himself, strangling* CLAUDIA *until she moves no more. When she is finally still, he looks at her and begins to weep, rocking her in his arms as the lights begin to fade. The sound of his sobs fill the room.)*

*(*WOLFGANG*'s cries of despair are heard as the lights fade. Lights up on* AMALIA *reading.)*

AMALIA. Dear Wolfgang,
    I never dreamt that...I never dreamt there was another

woman.

I thought it was just Germany for you.

Sometimes I couldn't look at you in Berlin,

during the trial and at other times....well,

there isn't always logic to what you feel is there?

(Lights up on **WOLFGANG** *appears and we see that he is now back in his prison cell. Then back to* **AMALIA.** *)*

I hear they're letting you wear your own clothes till they sentence you.

You don't have to wear the prison uniform. That's good.

I'm sending you your Mother's Star of David with this letter.

I thought you might need it now.

So...your lawyer's calling it a crime of passion. Passion for Germany,

for your Mother, and for...*her.* For the...for the singer.

I'm not sure though...really

Where does that leave me?

And you, Wolfgang. Where do you belong?

(The lights cross fade to **WOLFGANG** *as at the start of the play. He holds a Star of David in his hand.)*

WOLFGANG. Belong, Amalia?

(He turns toward her, then back.)

Where do I belong?

("Mother Have You Forgiven Me?" begins to play as the lights fade to black.)

END

PROPERTIES/FURNITURE LIST

Low chair or stool for Wolfgang in opening and closing scenes.
Work bench with hat blocks.
Kitchen/dining table.
Bed/sitting room furniture, however basic.
Cabaret table and microphone.
Numerous very high quality hats of various colours.

COSTUMES

NOTE: All authentic costumes are of the period.

CLAUDIA..Glamorous dress.
AMALIA...High-quality dress (more demure
than Claudia's.
WOLFGANG...............................Elegant. Double-breasted suit jacket,
waistcoat, shirt, tie and trilby.
GERHARDT..German officer uniform.
IRMGART (WOLFGANG'S MOTHER)......................Appropriately well-
dressed for a milliner.
FRAU HENDEL........................Elegant at first, then dowdy in Act Two.

AUTHOR'S NOTE ON SET PLOTS

Sets should be stark in both the opening and closing scenes.
When in the Cabaret, sets should be bright with the feel of decadence, then
faded a decadence.

MUSIC

(Here are the names of the songs and classical pieces below, in the order
in which they appear. This should be enough for directors to search for the
material.)

Mutter Hast Du Mir Vergeben
Unter den Linden.... Under the Linden ..
Brahms Hungarin Rapsody Number 5
"Falling in Love Again"
"La Vie en Rose."
Beeethoven's *Pathetitique*.
Be Careful of Blonde Women.   Vorsicht vor Blonden Frauen.
I Still Have a Suitcase in Berlin.... Ich habe noch einen Koffer in Berlin.
You Do Something to Me.